This book belongs to …

....

Tips for Talking and Reading Together

Stories are an enjoyable and reassuring way of introducing children to new experiences.

Before you read the story:

- Talk about the title and the picture on the cover. Ask your child what they think the story might be about.
- Talk about what a dentist is and what they do. Has your child ever been to the dentist with you?

Read the story with your child. After you have read the story:

- Discuss the Talk About ideas on page 27.
- Go through the tooth brushing instructions on pages 28 – 29.
- Do the fun activity on page 30.

Have fun!

Find the toothbrushes hidden in every picture.

For more hints and tips on helping your child become a successful and enthusiastic reader look at our website **www.oxfordowl.co.uk**.

Going to the Dentist

Written by Roderick Hunt
and Annemarie Young
Illustrated by Alex Brychta

OXFORD
UNIVERSITY PRESS

A man came to Kipper's class. He was
called Mr Molar. He made everyone laugh.

4

Mr Molar had a puppet. "This is Freddie Floss,"
he said.

"Hello, children," said the puppet in a funny voice.

"Oh dear!" said Mr Molar. "Look at Freddie's teeth."

"Ugh!" said everyone. "They're horrible."

The puppet had black spots on his teeth.
One tooth was missing.

"He hasn't been cleaning them properly," said Mr Molar.

"You must always clean your teeth properly," said Mr Molar.

"If you do, they will look like this!" he said.
The puppet's teeth were now shiny and white.

Kipper was playing with his yo-yo, and telling Mum about Mr Molar. He spun the yo-yo round very fast. Oh no! It hit him in the mouth.

He began to cry. "Is my tooth broken?" he asked.
"It really, really hurts."

11

"I don't think it's broken," said Mum, "but we should let the dentist look at it, just in case."

Kipper was worried. "Is it going to hurt?" he asked.

"Of course not," said Mum. "You'll like Mr Holland. He's good fun."

"This is my flying chair," said the dentist.
He let Kipper press the button and the chair
went up and down.

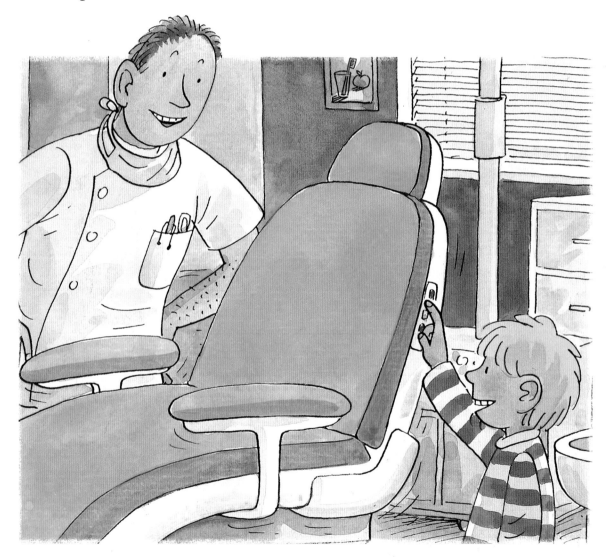

"Lie back in the flying chair," he said. "I'll just put this bright light on and look at your teeth."

15

"Your front tooth is fine," said Mr Holland. "But there's a little black spot on this back tooth."

"First I'm going to clean the spot. Then I'll
dry it and put a filling in it," he said.

"What is a black spot?" asked Kipper.

"It means the tooth is just starting to go bad,"
said Mr Holland.

"You can get holes in your teeth," he said, "if you
don't clean them every day, and if you eat lots of sweets."

Mum bought some tablets and some new toothbrushes.

"I'm going to clean my teeth properly from now on," said Kipper.

Kipper told Dad, Biff and Chip about the dentist. "I've got something for you," he said. He gave them each a tablet to chew.

Biff and Chip chewed the tablets, but they had
only a few red specks on their teeth.

"We clean them well," said Chip.

Dad began to go out of the room.

"Come back, Dad," called Kipper. "Show us your teeth."

"Hmmm!" said Dad.

"Oh Dad!" said Kipper. "Look at your red teeth!
I'll show you how to clean them properly."

Talk about the story

Why did the children say 'ugh!' when they saw Freddie Floss's teeth?

How did Kipper feel when he hurt his tooth?

Why did the dentist give Kipper a tablet to chew?

Have you ever hurt yourself? Who helped to make it better?

27

How to clean your teeth

Start with the outsides of your teeth –
first on the top, then on the bottom.

Put the brush like this, against your
teeth and gums.

Use small circular movements.
Don't scrub!

Then do the insides – first on the top,
then on the bottom.

You can hold the toothbrush like this when you do the insides.

Then clean the tops of your molars (the chewing surfaces). Here it is OK to scrub.

And then, to feel if they are clean, run your tongue over all your teeth. Rinse out and you're done!

Find the twins

Find the two pictures of Freddie that are exactly the same.

FIRST EXPERIENCES WITH Biff, Chip & Kipper

Have you read them all yet?

Kipper's First Pet

Learning to Swim

series created by Roderick Hunt and Alex Brychta

Going to the Dentist

Fun at the Farm

series created by Roderick Hunt and Alex Brychta

Going to the Doctor

series created by Roderick Hunt and Alex Brychta

Going to the Hairdresser

OXFORD

Going on a Plane

series created by Roderick Hunt and Alex Brychta

Starting School

OXFORD

series created by Roderick Hunt and Alex Brychta

FIRST EXPERIENCES Flashcards

55 cards

Also available:
- Kipper Gets Nits!
- At the Hospital
- At the Optician
- Bottles, Cans, Plastic Bags
- On a Train
- At the Vet
- At the Match
- At the Dance Class

Read with Biff, Chip and Kipper
The UK's best-selling home reading series

Phonics   First Stories

Level 1
Getting ready to read

Phonics stories help children practise their sounds and letters, as they learn to do in school.
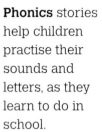

Level 2
Starting to read

First stories have been specially written to provide practice in reading everyday language.

Level 3
Becoming a reader

Level 4
Developing as a reader

Level 5
Building confidence in reading

Level 6
Reading with confidence

OXFORD
UNIVERSITY PRESS

Great Clarendon Street, Oxford OX2 6DP
Text © Roderick Hunt and Annemarie
Young 2007
Illustrations © Alex Brychta 2007
First published 2007
This edition published 2012

10 9 8 7 6 5 4 3 2 1
Series Editors: Kate Ruttle, Annemarie Young
British Library Cataloguing in Publication Data available
ISBN: 978-0-19-848794-4
Printed in China by Imago
The characters in this work are the original creation of Roderick
Hunt and Alex Brychta who retain copyright in the characters.
With thanks to Tony Holland BDS, LDS RCS